"Eat!"

Cried Little Pig

by Jonathan London

illustrated by Delphine Durand

Dutton Children's Books · New York

For **Baby Claire**, and for **Little Tyler**,
who cries, "Eat!"
–J.L.

For **Mateo, Lucien, Felix, Ismael,** and **Webster**
–D.D.

Text copyright © 2003 by Jonathan London
Illustrations copyright © 2003 by Delphine Durand
All rights reserved.

CIP Data is available.

Published in the United States by Dutton Children's Books,
a division of Penguin Young Readers Group
345 Hudson Street, New York, New York 10014
www.penguinputnam.com

Designed by Gloria Cheng

Manufactured in China
First Edition
ISBN 0-525-46906-0
1 3 5 7 9 10 8 6 4 2

"EAT!" cried Little Pig.

("Eat" was his first word.)

"EAT!" cried Little Pig.

So Mama Pig
gave him
breakfast...

and Little Pig ate.
He ate **off** his plate,

and he ate **on** his plate!

Squish went the banana.
Squash went the eggs.
Squish-squash went everything
that landed on his legs.

Food in his hair.
Food on his chair.
Food on his clothes
and food everywhere!

At lunchtime...

"EAT!"

cried Little Pig.

"Be sweet,"
said his sister.

And Little Pig ate.
He ate his whole plate.
His appetite was great!

Slurp went the noodles.
Slop went the milk.
There were oodles of noodles
and puddles of milk.

Food in
his hair.

Food
on his
teddy bear.

Food on
the floor

and food
everywhere!

"Stop it!" cried his sister.
"EAT!" cried Little Pig.
He grabbed his sister's plate
and ate and ate and ate...
till he fell off his chair.

At dinnertime...

"EAT!" cried Little Pig. "Be neat," said Papa Pig.

And Little Pig ate.

He ate with all his might.

He ate everything in sight!

Mish went the beans.
Mash went the peas.
Mish-mash went everything
that landed on his knees.

Food in his hair.
Food in the air.
Food on the ceiling
    and food
        everywhere!

It slid down the walls
and flew from the fan.
It was rolled into balls
and spilled from the pan.

It oozed and it dripped,
it bumped and it thumped,

till Papa Pig slipped...

and fell

on his rump!

The cat licked and lapped,
and Little Pig clapped.

The dog licked and wiggled,
and Little Pig giggled.

"What a mess!" cried his papa.
"What a mess!"

"He's still a baby," sighed his mama,
and helped him undress.

She scrubbed
his nose.

She scrubbed
his hair.

She scrubbed his clothes and washed his chair.

She got him dressed
and said, "Time to rest."

But when she tiptoed out...

she heard a shout:
"EAT!" cried Little Pig.
"Oh no!" cried Mama Pig.

"NEAT!" cried Little Pig.
("Neat" was his second word.)

So Mama Pig gave him dessert...

and Little Pig ate.

No food in his hair.
No food on his underwear.
No food in his bed.

No food **anywhere!**

"SWEET!" he said
("Sweet" was his third word)
and threw his toys instead.